THIS WALKER BOOK BELONGS TO:

_____

_____

_____

For Daniel, Katarina and Hill

First published 2004 by Walker Books Ltd
87 Vauxhall Walk, London SE11 5HJ

This edition published 2005

10 9 8 7 6 5 4 3 2 1

© 2004 Sue Heap

The right of Sue Heap to be identified as author/illustrator
of this work has been asserted by her in accordance with
the Copyright, Designs and Patents Act 1988

This book has been typeset in Tiffany

Printed in China

British Library Cataloguing in Publication Data:
a catalogue record for this book is available
from the British Library

ISBN 1-84428-554-5

www.walkerbooks.co.uk

Four Friends in the Garden

Sue Heap

WALKER BOOKS

AND SUBSIDIARIES

LONDON • BOSTON • SYDNEY • AUCKLAND

One sunny day
the four friends
are in the garden.

Florentina the bear is gently swinging.
Rachel the rabbit is nibbling clover.
Mary Clare is making daisy-chains.
Seymour the sheep is sitting on his hill.

"Ooof!" says Florentina. "I am hot." She kicks off her slippers.

A butterfly lands
on her foot.
"Aaah!" she sighs.
"How beautiful!"

"Rachel, Seymour, Mary Clare," calls Florentina.
"Look! A butterfly has landed on me!"
 She waits with her foot in the air.
 The butterfly shivers its wings …

and flies away.

"What butterfly?" asks Seymour.
"Where?" asks Rachel.
"Was it on your foot?" asks Mary Clare.

"There it goes!" calls Florentina, and she gets up and runs towards the lemon tree.
The others come running after her.

"There it goes!" calls Florentina,
and she runs towards the rose bushes.
The others come running after her.

"There it goes!" calls Florentina again.
But Seymour is hot and cross.
"There is no butterfly," he says, stopping.

"I can't see it," says Rachel.
"Why does it keep going away?"
asks Mary Clare.

Seymour goes back to sit on his hill.
Mary Clare and Rachel go too.
For a moment they're all quiet together.

Then the butterfly lands on Seymour's hand.
"Aaah!" they all say. "How beautiful!"
The butterfly shivers its wings ...

and flies away.

Seymour, Rachel and Mary Clare run round and round the garden.

But now,
where is the butterfly ...
and where is Florentina?

"Here are her slippers," says Rachel.
"She's gone," says Mary Clare.
"Like the butterfly," says Seymour.

And then they hear ...

"Yoo-hoo! Lemonade!"

and Florentina is back,
carrying a tray with
a jug and four cups.

They sit in the grass and
drink iced lemonade together.
"Four friends in the garden," says Seymour,
"one, two, three, four."
Just then the butterfly lands on Florentina's nose.
"Five," whispers Florentina.
"What a lovely day!"

WALKER BOOKS is the world's leading
independent publisher of children's books.
Working with the best authors and illustrators
we create books for all ages, from babies
to teenagers – books your child will
grow up with and always remember. So…

FOR THE BEST CHILDREN'S BOOKS,
LOOK FOR THE BEAR